Beauty Touched the Beast

Skye Warren

Praise for the Beauty series

"I love this 'Beauty and the Beast' story that Skye Warren has crafted. She puts a twist to this classic tale that makes it different and deliciously erotic."

—Nina's Literary Escape

"Skye weaves emotion and eroticism together in such a fantastic way. Beauty Becomes You is no exception. I'm going to miss these two – especially Blake's raw way of making love *wink* – but at least there are always rereads."

—Romantic Book Affairs

"Loved this version of Beauty and the Beast. What a clever, sexy, and inventive way to recreate this classic tale."

—Sir's kitten

"I love a scarred hero and Blake was perfect in every way. I even loved his vulnerabilities and wanted to hug him tight."

—Punya's Reviews

"An intriguing and sexy beastly hero, a vulnerable young student who coaxes him out of his shell, and a romantic and erotic storyline that is sure to satisfy readers. Another winner from Warren."

—Penelope's Romance Reviews

"I consider this series a Top Pick because their story is not only very memorable and extremely sexy, but I could read this series many times over and never tire of it. In fact, I already know I will revisit them again for years to come."

—Ms Romantic Reads

CHAPTER ONE

ERIN JOGGED UP the steps of the farm-style house in good spirits.

She let herself in using her key and called out, "Mr. Morris! It's Erin."

Call me Blake, he always asked, but for some reason she resisted. She wasn't usually a stickler for propriety, but with him it seemed like a good idea. Maybe his military roots made the formality more correct to her. Or more likely, it was the domesticity of cleaning his home while he loitered near her.

It would be so easy to slip, to let him see how she felt about him. Then she'd feel like an idiot—a dumb, little girl panting after a man old enough to be her father.

She pulled a book from her bag and went upstairs in search of her boss to return it to him. She could probably put it in his bookcase, always neat and organized so she'd know right where it belonged. In fact, his whole house sparkled from the knotted floorboards to the arched ceilings.

It was partly because he was so fastidious, but also because she did a full deep clean twice a week. It was one of the odd habits that made her reclusive employer so strange, and also endearing.

She could replace the book, but she wanted an excuse to talk to him. They'd had a lively debate on the merits of the U.N. in her political science class yesterday and she knew he'd appreciate it.

She poked her head in his bedroom and found him there. Her breath caught in her throat as she took in the sight. He lay spread out on the bed, his skin still damp from a bath, a towel in disarray around his waist.

And he was masturbating. *Shit!*

She ought to leave. This was clearly a private moment and she the intruder. She really should turn around, walk away and absolutely, positively not watch. Instead she stood there, her eyes riveted to his exposed cock standing up thick from his fisted hand.

"God, baby," he moaned, his eyes closed, "Suck it, please."

Her lips parted in surprise, as if she could obey him from across the room. Her clit throbbed to hear his rasping voice say those dirty words, to watch his fist fuck his cock.

"Yes. *Yesss.* So beautiful. God." His other hand reached to cup his balls. "That's right, baby. Lick them. Suck them."

Her wide-eyed gaze flew to his face, mesmerized by the interplay of shiny, scar tissue and ruddy, healthy skin twisted in a grimace of pleasure. His burns and coarse features might make him repulsive to some, but when she looked at him she saw only Blake, with his brilliant ideas and gruff kindness.

"Touch yourself. Yeah, yeah. Take me deep in your mouth and stick your fingers in your cunt."

Her thighs squeezed together where she stood, giving herself whatever relief she could. If she moved, either her legs or her hands, she'd have to acknowledge that what she was doing, that being a voyeur was wrong, so she stayed still instead.

Then, shockingly, he moaned her name, "Erin…"

Erin barely had time to process that, and then he came, spurting into his cupped hand.

More than a little turned on, she let out an involuntary sound—a whimper, almost. Heavy lids slid open as he turned to look at her. His eyes widening into a look of shock, even horror.

Mortified, she turned and ran down the stairs. The sound of her name hurtled down the steps after her, not in passion this time, but she couldn't go back.

Pacing in the kitchen, she battled her embarrassment at being caught in a compromising position. Or rather, she'd caught *him* in a compromising position. But since it was his house, and she just cleaned it for him, she'd messed up big time. She'd have to face him and apologize, but she couldn't look for him in his bedroom. Not right then and maybe not ever.

Her hands caught on the stone edge of the countertops, then flitted across the surface. Already clean, as usual. She'd never done anything quite this embarrassing. Watching the man's private moment? That was low.

And even worse, she respected him, so much. She *liked* him, and she might have ruined everything.

She pulled out the cleaning supplies, thinking that at least she could subvert her nervous energy into something useful. She'd come here to clean, not to moon after Blake and certainly not be a peeping Tom.

Blake bounded down the stairs soon after, wearing his customary sweats. She'd admired him before, the way the loose, comfortable clothing hung on his well-built shoulders and abs, but now all she could see was his naked, damp body. As if she hadn't already proven herself enough of a coward, she turned away as if to flee.

"Erin," he said in those low tones that always made her clench. "Wait, please."

She paused and turned halfway back to him, willing the inappropriate, private, *sexy* images to subside. A reddened cock. Thick ropes of come. *Dammit.*

"I'm sorry you had to see that," he said. "Don't … quit. It won't happen again. Please," he said.

She'd never expected to see him like this, practically begging—not for anything, and certainly not for his maid to continue cleaning for him. Did she really vacuum so well?

But no, if nothing else, today had shown that he at least *thought* about her in another way. Is *that* why he kept her around, why he increased her cleaning schedule and chatted with her about his work? Should she be offended?

But she wasn't. She was flattered. And turned on as

hell.

She stammered, "I don't understand. Were you…was I…?"

He closed his eyes and lowered his head. "There's no excuse," he said, swallowing. "But I won't—" He broke off and looked away. The part of his face turned toward her was the more scarred half. That gesture more than anything showed his distress since he usually took pains to hide it when possible.

"What can I do so that you will not leave?" he asked.

"I—honestly, I hadn't even thought of that. Actually, I wanted to apologize. For intruding on your privacy. I'm not going to quit."

"Thank you," he said stiffly, either in acknowledgement of her apology or her agreement she didn't know. He paused then repeated, "I'm sorry." After a curt nod, he disappeared into his study.

She thought maybe she should have told him that he didn't have anything to be sorry for, that he hadn't done anything wrong, after all. But it would be too strange to correct him in his assumption. What could she say? *Please, go ahead and use me in your fantasies. I don't mind.* That would hardly make this situation less awkward.

Besides, she needed time to think, to process what she had seen him do and her feelings. But she'd just committed not to quit, whatever came of her thoughts.

She cleaned his house as usual and he made himself scarce the rest of the time. She left his bedroom for last and resolutely ignored the way her panties grew damp as she made his bed.

✧ ✧ ✧

THANK GOD SHE *hadn't quit*, he thought, as he fled to the study.

He'd known she'd arrive any minute and he hadn't been unable to deflate his erection with a cold shower. He'd had to take care of it before she arrived. She couldn't see his inappropriate desire for her. It would ruin everything. But he'd miscalculated, and badly.

Of all the ways to lose her, that would've been the stupidest. Not that he *had* her, exactly, but seeing her twice a week and getting to talk with her was more than he deserved, and he was damned grateful for it. He chose not to analyze the pathetic factor of that.

It was sleazy of him to use her work to bring him to his house—he'd never had such a clean house in his life—but he could think of no other way to keep her around him. Someone so beautiful and good had no business being around a pissy coward like himself, but damned if he wasn't selfish enough to force her anyways. Lord knew he had no good looks, no charm, and as evidenced by earlier, no intelligence with which to lure her instead.

The great intellectual, he thought in disgust, thinking with his dick. Not that he didn't excuse himself to a certain extent—Lord, she was beautiful. Seeing her watching his dick while he'd come had only inflamed his lust for her, but it was best not to think on that lest he require a repeat performance.

It was bad enough to be scarred and ugly, broken in body and spirit, wasn't it? Surely he didn't need to add creepy old exhibitionist to his faults.

Chapter Two

ONE HOUR INTO her next cleaning visit, Erin was getting worried. She'd hoped everything could go back to normal, but Blake still seemed to be avoiding her. He'd made a brief appearance to say hello and that was it. He didn't sit on the couch as she folded the clothes or lean against the bookshelves while she dusted. He didn't tell her about what book he was writing, what article he was researching, not asking her about her classes. Nothing like usual.

Today he wore jeans and a button-up shirt. He always went around his house in sweats, the super comfy kind, thin from frequent wearing and washing. He worked from home and almost never ventured outside. Plus he eschewed such society-imposed discomforts as regular clothes.

She could only assume this new formality was in reaction to the incident from last week. Perhaps he felt violated or unsafe with her, and although she didn't blame him, she felt horribly guilty.

It didn't help that she'd had explicit dreams about him and his cock two nights in a row. Dreams where he said those same words, but she was there, naked beside him, and she did what he asked. Masturbating to thoughts of each other was a contagious condition, one she'd now caught, she thought dryly.

He ducked out of the kitchen with a glass of water as she entered it. Concerned and, exasperated, she decided to confront him.

"Mr. Morris," she called. When he froze, she softened her voice, "Blake, I wanted to apologize again for what happened last time. I should have left right away when I saw what you were doing…well, I was just surprised," she explained.

He looked surprised now, too. He cleared his throat. "Apology accepted."

He flashed her what was she supposed was a conciliatory smile but looked more like a grimace. And *that* made her think of what he looked like when he climaxed. *Dammit.*

She really should shut up now, but she couldn't seem to stop. "I was wondering if you, that is, if you *were* thinking of me…weren't you?" she asked.

His eyes widened even as his lips tightened.

"Well, it's only that, I wondered if… if it was just a passing thought or if it was more …" She trailed off.

He looked alarmed now and she cursed herself silently. "Erin," he said, his voice strangled. "You don't feel that I was asking you to do anything… inappropriate, do you? That I would try to make you do something—something you didn't want?"

"No!" she exclaimed in dismay. "Of course not. I just

meant that, well, if you *were* interested in me that way, well, I—" She took a deep breath and rushed out, "I wouldn't necessarily be opposed to it."

"You—" He broke off. She noticed detachedly that his hand was gripping the counter so tight his knuckles were white. He swayed forward as if to approach her but then leaned back. "Are you sure? Are you sure you don't feel pressured? I would never *ever* want you to feel that you had to—"

"No, no. It's not that, I swear. And the same goes for you, too. If you don't want to, *please* don't feel that you must—"

"If I don't want to," he repeated, sounding dazed. His eyes unfocused for a minute, and then pinned her. He stepped forward and then circled around, standing behind her. Her hair rustled and scalp tingled where his face leaned into her hair, as if he were scenting her.

He trailed a finger lightly from the crown of her head, down her hair, along her shoulder and her arm. It wasn't an overtly sexual touch, but she found it highly erotic. The past two days of heightened arousal boiled over in her until she felt strung out with need.

"Please," she whimpered, shocked at herself even as she said it. She considered herself a proud woman, probably to her detriment. Her circumstances, cleaning houses while her classmates drove their Mercedes to class, ought to bring her down, but she would not be cowed. She was like him—she never begged, not for anything, money, favor and certainly not sex. Yet here she was wanting—no, *needing* him, a feeling foreign but very real.

Thankfully, he acquiesced.

"God, yes," he breathed into her hair. "Come. Come upstairs where you can be more comfortable." He led her upstairs to his room. She noticed dust gathered in a corner on the way and reality intruded briefly—*that's what I'm here to do, to clean his house, not have sex*—but she forced it away. It had been a long time for her and she needed this badly. She would take this moment without apology to herself or anyone else.

In the bedroom he shut the door. No one else was in the house but the two of them, but it added to the intimacy of the moment. This wasn't a chance encounter, but an illicit meeting. She stood eyeing the bed and swallowed hard. He came up behind her and again buried his face in her hair. Amused, she made a mental note to stock up on this shampoo. But then the heat of his body and his own woodsy scent enveloped her, and she forgot everything else.

His hands rested lightly on her shoulders, then slid down to her breasts. He cupped them through her clothing and her breath caught. The gentle caress dipped down to her waist and then up under her shirt and bra to touch bare skin. She wore yoga clothes when cleaning, comfortable to maneuver in but stretchy enough to allow him access.

He cupped her breasts, stroking and pinching her nipples until they ached. Pausing to draw her shirt and bra up over her head, he returned his hands to her breasts—thank God. His breath, hot and increasingly labored, blew against her shoulder. What a sight she must have made for him, her breasts bared and flushed.

"So lovely," he whispered.

When he pinched harder, she moaned. Her hips canted forward in search of friction, rubbing against nothing. In answer to her involuntary plea, he slipped his hand into the waistband of her pants and roamed lower until he found her wet folds.

As his hands touched her intimately, his mouth found the skin of her neck in light kisses and licks. He dipped down to her opening to draw the moisture up to her clit, circling and flicking with his thumb. Her head fell back to his chest and her eyes closed as she abandoned herself to the pleasure. His fingers slid down into her folds and slipped inside, thrusting his fingers in as the heel of his hand pushed into her clit. Her hips bucked as she mindlessly sought climax.

She came in a whirl of pleasure and a sigh of relief. Her body fell back against him, sated. The tension of these past few days, of these past few months, if she were honest, finally released.

He undressed her completely and placed her on the bed. She had no strength to stop him. No desire to. By the time she floated back down to earth she lay spread eagle on the bed, completely naked, with him kneeling between her legs. She only had a glimpse of his scarred face, taut and carnal with arousal, before he lowered his head and brought her to ecstasy again.

He was a generous lover, bringing her to climax four, five times—she lost count. He made her come again and again with his mouth on her clit and his fingers thrusting inside her.

"Yes, yes, that's it," he would moan when she came.

He was relentless in his pursuit of her orgasms, taking unmistakable pleasure in her sounds and responsiveness. She was reminded of how they would discuss topics related to his work or her college classes. He always argued fiercely and often won their debates, but when she would win, he wouldn't look disappointed or angry—he looked almost proud. Triumphant, even. Like her victory was his, and now her ecstasy was his, too.

"You're beautiful," he murmured to her throughout. "So damn beautiful. You look like a goddess. Like a warrior. Like you could slay me and you *do*. Just looking at you ruins me. I love to look at you. I could look at you lying spread like this forever. Open to me, wet and flushed—forever and never grow tired."

She'd read his articles and treatises and interviews. He had plain-spoken words and clinical words and words of dry humor, but she had never heard these words before. These almost-poetry sex/love words melted her everywhere.

Her body throbbed, exhausted from her climaxes, but her heart burst from his generosity. She wanted to do something for him. She wanted to do everything for him.

Erin reached down and grasped his cock, drawing a gasp from him. The pulsing shaft jerked in her hand but he pulled away. From her position she couldn't reach him in his retreat. He touched her again and she jumped, oversensitive.

"Just let me please you," he said. "Let me give you pleasure." His caress lightened. She moaned and her legs relaxed open again.

"Yes," he murmured. "Yes, that's right. Good girl."

His fingers spread apart her folds, slick and swollen.

"I'll make you feel so much pleasure," he said. "So much you won't care that it's me."

Wait, what? She tried to push through the haze of her arousal.

"So good you'll forget it's me," he whispered, staring down at her spread legs, entranced. "You won't regret this. I won't let you regret this," he promised.

"Stop," she gasped out and he snatched his hand back. "What—what did you say?"

He shook his head and some of the sensual fog cleared from his eyes. "I'm sorry," he said. "Did you…did you want to stop? Are you finished?"

"No, I don't want to stop," she said. "I want to keep doing this with you. With *you!*"

She sighed in exasperation.

"Lie down," she commanded.

He blinked in surprise but obeyed. Without giving him a chance to reject her, she reached down and grasped his cock again. She sucked him into her mouth.

"Oh God, *yes*," he cried, just as he had when he'd pleasured himself with her on his mind. But this time was real and she'd make sure he knew it.

She savored the tangy flavor of his semen as it hit her tongue, and breathed in deep the musky, male smell of his groin. His thighs shook. All this power and virility trembled under her mouth. It intoxicated her.

She took him in deep and then pulled back to the tip. In and out. Deeper and deeper.

The rhythmic motions of his cock sliding back and forth between her lips felt like a chant. This man was so good and so kind and yet, was it possible that he questioned his worth because of his scars? It was ludicrous. Those scars, received in battle as a soldier, proved his bravery and honor. It was another example of him protecting others, the way he advocated for unheard groups and causes in his writing.

How dare anyone—how dare *he*—question his value? He was everything she could ever want in a man.

She loved him.

What the hell? Where had that thought come from?

Her eyes snapped open in surprise only to find him staring at her intently, as if he could devour her with sight alone. He looked fierce and sexy and intimidating. Her eyes widened at the hunger in his eyes.

Through his arousal, he managed a small smile and touched her cheek tenderly. "It's okay," he said softly. "You don't have to look."

He thought she didn't want to look at him, to see his

beautiful face? He thought she wanted to pretend it was someone else licking her, pleasuring her?

She grew angry. Angry at him for doubting himself. He doubted her, too, thinking her that shallow. She was angry at the faceless people who had wounded him, outside and in.

It didn't have to be like that. She'd show him so. Even if this afternoon was all she had with him, he'd know his worth.

She retaliated by tightening her lips and sucking hard. He bucked his hips and groaned, eyes sliding closed helplessly.

She continued her onslaught using strong suction and steady thrusts. She took him in deep, too deep. She was practically stabbing her throat, impaling her mouth with his cock, but she didn't care. She sucked and fucked him that way as hard as she could, as if his cock was her lifeline and maybe it was.

He thrust his hips up jerkily, mindlessly trying to get deeper, push farther. She tried to oblige him, jamming her head down onto him, her lips grazing the hair at the base. And that groan rumbled all the way into her throat. She could have come from the sound alone, if her hands had been free to touch herself, but they weren't. His cock choked her, but it seemed insignificant compared to *this*.

When it was over he lay in a post-orgasmic stupor, reaching his hand down for her, seeking connection. She felt a similar sated haze seep into her. She clambered up his body and curled herself up at the crook of his arm.

CHAPTER THREE

B LAKE WASN'T GOING to jump her next time she came over. At the very least, it was sexual harassment, what he had done. His mind had even drifted to worse these past few days. What if she hadn't wanted it? What if she'd felt that she couldn't say no? It would have been practically rape.

Either way, he should be arrested. Beaten. Someone should kick his ass for taking advantage of her. It was too damned bad that Erin didn't have anyone to beat the shit out of him. No father, no brothers, no punk-ass college boyfriend, either. She was vulnerable, and he'd been the worst kind of bastard.

When she came in the front door, she called out like she always did. "Mr. Morris, it's Erin."

His pulse jumped at her voice. His cock hardened. God, no.

He couldn't do this. Bad enough she knew he was a dirty old man, taking advantage, lusting after her. Worse that he'd used her own desperation, her need to work to pay for her college, as a tether to keep her near him. He couldn't also take her body, her innocence.

For she *was* innocent. Oh, she'd had sex before. And

Christ, she'd sucked his dick like he'd never experienced it. Not even before his injuries had he gotten it so good. But her brown eyes were so open, so trusting. Her body was lithe and smooth and young. He didn't deserve any of it.

There it was, entering the kitchen. That incredible body and beautiful mind.

"Erin," he said. "We have to talk."

She picked up on his tone correctly, setting her face into solemn lines, but then she'd always been bright. She walked to him, keeping her eyes trained to his. Probably she was worried he'd touch her again, put his filthy hands on her body and his ugly face near hers. And why shouldn't she be? He was an animal.

"I'm afraid this isn't going to work," he said. "You can't work here anymore."

"Okay," she said, sounding calm. But her hands trembled. And when she saw that he'd noticed, she clamped them together. She wasn't one to show her weakness, and he hated that he'd made her weak.

"You understand, this isn't any fault of yours," he said. "You've done a great job. I've never had such a clean house. It's just…well, I'm sure you realize the problem. It can't happen again."

"Right," she said in that same neutral tone. "I under-stand."

He didn't want to hurt her, but he could see that he had. He'd thought maybe she'd be a little disappointed, since he liked to think they'd had a friendship. Or maybe she'd be relieved that she could get away from the lecher without him making a fuss. That would have been bad, but this was far worse.

But he knew what it was. "I realize you rely on this job for college. I don't intend to ruin that for you. I can give you some money. The same amount you would have made it you'd kept working here."

Her facade cracked. So did her voice. "You want to pay me?"

"Well, yes," he said, genuinely confused by her distress. He'd done her wrong, by having sex with her. He'd pay the price, all right, not getting to see her again. But the least he could do was leave her whole, and that meant paying her the wages she would have earned.

She stood. Her lower lip trembled, but her eyes flashed with anger. "You can keep your goddamn money."

"Erin, I don't understand—"

"You don't understand? I'll explain it to you. I know I'm just some stupid college kid and you don't really care. I can accept that. I'm just a maid to you, and a girl you can fuck, fine. But I am not a whore. You can't have sex with me and then pay me to go away."

He was shocked. "I didn't mean it like that. Of course you're not a whore."

Her face crumpled at the last word. She turned and ran from the room. He caught up to her as she grabbed her purse from the hallway table, fumbling inside for her keys.

He stayed her arm. "Erin. Erin, please."

She couldn't see what she was doing through her tears, and she dropped the bag in frustration, but she refused to look up at him.

"Erin, I'm sorry," he said. "I never should have touched you. You deserve so much better than—"

"Oh, don't give me that," she cried, finally turning up her tear stained cheeks to him. "You know I'd give anything to be with you. I'd take it any way you could give it to me, but not if you're going to *pay* me for it. I can't be a prostitute, even for you."

"I don't want that," he said. "I want you, that's all. I just can't have you. You're so beautiful, so young, and I—"

"Shhh," she said. "That's it. That's all we need to say to each other. If you meant what you said, if you really want me, then that's enough for me."

"Well, it shouldn't be," he said, angry now. "You should have standards. You should—"

Then his voice strangled as she grabbed the hem of her shirt and pulled it over her head.

Her sports bra was barely fabric at all, showing her tight nipples. Her abs sloped into wide hips, encased in tight black pants. His mouth went dry.

Warning bells clanged in his head. He'd said he wasn't going to do this, wasn't going to touch her, that he didn't get to have her. But then she pulled off the bra, too, and his brain blissfully shut off.

He couldn't help it. With a groan of resignation, of

appreciation, he pulled her into his arms for a slow, languorous kiss. This was happening. Whatever came after would be on his head, but for now he had to taste her, to feel her beneath him, to pretend.

Beautiful, beautiful. He wanted to touch her in all those beautiful places, but that was everywhere. Her full lips, but no, that was for his mouth to explore. And those breasts, plump and tipped with bronze—they were for his mouth.

But lower was the soft, feminine curve of her stomach, all sleek lines and sloping shadows. And even lower, the satiny softness of her sex, but he couldn't touch them all. Not at once, and that's what his mind was consumed with, now, now. Touch her now, take her now. *She's mine now.*

Too late, he noticed her hand pressing against his chest, stopping him. She wanted him to stop.

Yes, he would. Of course he would. He would never force himself on anyone, and especially not her. Not his ugly face or his too-old body.

But she wasn't really stopping him, he saw. She took him by the hand and led him to the bedroom. Kicking off her pants, she crawled up onto the bed. Her legs were parted in that haphazard way of a woman. Sprawling in invitation but tilted closed with modesty.

Before he could process any reasons why he shouldn't, he was naked on top of her. A crazed man. He licked and sucked and *bit*. She should stop him, the small rational part of his brain cried. But that was doused by her heat and his.

She gave it all back to him. Touching him, tasting him.

Her mouth worked its way down and he wanted that—God, did he. But he also didn't think he could last. He knew he couldn't, so he stopped her.

"Baby," he said, and she stopped and looked at him. He nudged her shoulder, not able to get out more words than just that. *Baby*. She was his.

AT HIS URGING, Erin rolled to her hands and knees. Yes. This way, that way. The position didn't matter, so long as he got inside her, in her mouth or *somewhere*. She was frantic with it, with the need to hold him in her body.

The sharp tear of the wrapper, a short pause and then he was in. His cock thrust into her from behind. His thick body covered her back while his mouth whispered in her ear.

"Baby, you're so hot. Do you know how much I want you? All I can think about. You make me stupid. Mine, mine."

It felt good. It did. But…she thought back to the first time and what he had said.

You don't have to look.

Is that what he was doing? Making it so she didn't have to see him?

And she wanted to see him. More than that, she didn't want him to think she didn't.

She started to turn, but he put a strong hand on her back.

"Not good?" he panted.

She could feel him changing the angle and—ahh!—yes, that *was* better. That wasn't the point though. That wasn't the problem.

She jerked away so he had no choice but to let her go or restrain her. He let her go. He always would, she knew that. He would always be gentle with her. Without giving him a chance to think, to pull away, she flipped over, spread her legs and guided his cock inside her. His eyes widened, as if he might protest, but then they slid shut.

He moaned, long and low. "So good. Mine."

She wanted to smile at that—she loved when he said that. She never wanted him to stop saying it, but she couldn't smile at all. Not when the pressure, the tension, the joy of it was building, higher and higher. She could hardly breathe, much less smile, and then she'd reached the top. She came with a strangled cry and he followed after, pumping into her and carrying her orgasm until she was wrung out.

"Erin," he mumbled into her hair, "Don't leave. Don't ever leave… love you."

He froze. She could almost hear him thinking—first replaying what he'd just said and then searching for something to say.

She cupped his cheek in her hand. It was the one that fit her free hand, but it happened to be the damaged one, the scarred one, and she stroked her thumb over the too-smooth, discolored skin.

"Love you, too," she whispered.

He groaned and shut his eyes, turning his face into her touch.

THE END

Thank You!

Thank you for reading Beauty Touched the Beast!

- Originally Blake and Erin's story stopped here, but I had more readers request sequels than for any other work. By overwhelming demand, their story continues in a series of novellas starting with Beneath the Beauty. Or get the Beauty series compilation.

- Would you like to know when my next book is released? You can sign up for my newsletter at skyewarren.com/newsletter.

- Like me on Facebook at facebook.com/skyewarren.

- I appreciate your help in spreading the word, including telling a friend.

- Reviews help readers find books! Leave a review on your favorite book site.

- Turn the page for a short excerpt from Beneath the Beauty…

Beneath the Beauty

"An intriguing and sexy beastly hero, a vulnerable young student who coaxes him out of his shell, and a romantic and erotic storyline that is sure to satisfy readers."

—Penelope's Romance Reviews

When Blake receives an offer to return to his alma mater as an associate professor, he knows this is his chance to reenter the world—and to be worthy of the woman he loves. Erin wants this chance for him to heal…even if it means leaving her behind.

"Skye Warren delivers a some very sensual, sexy scenes."

—Fiction Vixen

EXCERPT FROM
BENEATH THE BEAUTY

ERIN WOKE UP in slow degrees. Awareness tugged at her like a gentle tide. Arousal lapped at her skin. She had been in a deep slumber, both sated and sore, but she came alive again under his touch.

Blake. Sighing, she might have said his name aloud. Or maybe just in her mind. They were attuned now, so soon after sex. Wrapped up in each other, cocooned in sleep. Past the point of discussions, negotiations, they'd been stripped to the core. Just him, her, and the pleasure they could invoke together.

Calloused fingers roamed over her hips and lower, lower, to where her curls were still damp from their earlier sex. She peeked at the windows. A faint, eerie light glowed against the curtains, heralding late twilight, the onslaught of night. He was insatiable really. Earlier this evening, then now. They'd do it again in the morning most likely. She loved it.

When his fingers slipped inside the wetness pooling at her sex, she moaned.

"Shh. I didn't mean to wake you."

Liar. A lazy smile curved her lips. "Is that right?"

He found her clit and pinched. His breath was hot at the back of her neck, his erection pressing urgently against her from behind. "But now that you're up…"

"You have plans for me." Delicious plans. They always were.

"You don't have to do a thing," he murmured, rolling her onto her back. He nuzzled his way through the valley of her breasts, across her belly, and settled in between her legs. Her knees splayed wide, her whole body spread open to him, encouraged by anticipation and the laxity of sleep. Her hips canted up, an instinctual invitation.

She'd been given oral sex before, but never by someone as dedicated as Blake. He enjoyed himself there as much as he enjoyed regular sex—maybe more. He could make her come endless times, until she was throbbing and restless, until she had to beg him to come inside her.

God, she loved it.

Two weeks wasn't a long time, but she felt incredibly close to Blake. She trusted him with her body—and hell, with her heart. She had dated her last boyfriend for eight months without feeling this level of intimacy. He certainly had never done *this* to her, lapping from the bottom to the top, lingering in a lazy circle around her clit, pressing in an instinctual rhythm until her hips took up the beat.

Before she could climax, he licked and sucked his way lower. His tongue slipped between her lips, sparking tendrils of need through her core.

"Oh, Blake," she moaned, lost to the sensations, shuddering on the edge.

"What is it, baby?" he murmured against her flesh. "Tell me what you want. Take what you need."

She fisted his hair and guided his mouth to her clit. He eagerly sucked her there, using his lips and tongue to drive her higher and further until she was taut, stretched out, and ready to burst.

It was the touch of his fingers to her inner lips that pushed her over, a tickle of a caress combined with the harsh pleasure at her clit, and she came in a sunburst that belied the heavy shadows surrounding them.

Slowly coming down, she blinked up at the ceiling, feeling energized. "Now I'm well and truly awake."

"Shit," he said, sounding dismayed.

"It's not a complaint, mister. That was amazing."

"Don't worry." He lowered his mouth to her sex. "I think we can wear you out all over again."

She would have smiled then, but his tongue curled wickedly and his fingers delved deeper. Her thighs drew up tight, and she came again, smaller this time, in tense, rolling waves. He didn't give her a reprieve, just set the flat of his tongue against her clit, which was at once too sensitive and exactly what she needed. She grew louder, her body writhing without her control, but each new orgasm sent her farther into the sex-drugged space.

When her body shuddered in one final orgasm, he knelt between her legs. She noticed distantly that his hands were shaking as he put on the condom, as he angled his cock at her slippery cunt and pushed inside. It was all wonderful but never more than that moment, when she felt so full and watched an expression of bliss soothe his tortured face.

On the one side, his skin was smooth, aside from the ruggedness and bristle of an active, healthy man. The flesh on the other side had once been burned, ravaged by fire and war, now covered with scar tissue. It hurt to see, but only because she ached for him, for the pain he must have felt in that moment, for the pain that kept him locked up in his immaculate house instead of out in the world.

To her he was beautiful. In the moonlight, the jagged landscape of his scars was more pronounced. But it was his slack jaw that she admired, his glazed eyes. The signs of his ecstasy brought on by her body. As if he were a god, she offered herself up to him, but it wasn't a sacrifice to feel the heavy weight of his muscles, the thick pulse of his cock, the tender press of his lips against her when he bent to drop a kiss. He thrust inside her, faster and harder, pushing them onward in a sea of molten pleasure.

"Shit," he muttered. "I can't—I can't—"

"Don't hold back." Then she repeated his earlier words. "Take what you need."

They seemed to release him. He picked up speed, slamming inside her so hard it took her breath away. He pressed his lips to hers, moving his tongue to the same rhythm as his hips. He invaded her at both places, her mouth and her sex, and held her down in all the rest, but she wouldn't have moved for the world. She longed for him to take her, to use her. Anything she could do to bring him pleasure. Anything to bring him peace.

His hips lost their steady motion, jerking up against her like waves on a cliff, crashing until he let out a hoarse shout and held still for his climax.

Want to read more? Beneath the Beauty is available now Amazon.com, iBooks, BarnesAndNoble.com and other retailers. Or you can get the Beauty series compilation.

Other Books by Skye Warren

Wanderlust

On the Way Home

Hear Me

Prisoner

Dark Nights Series

Keep Me Safe (prequel)

Trust in Me

Don't Let Go

The Beauty Series

Beauty Touched the Beast

Beneath the Beauty

Broken Beauty

Beauty Becomes You

The Beauty Series Compilation

Standalone Erotic Romance

His for Christmas

Take the Heat: A Criminal Romance Anthology

Sweetest Mistress

Below the Belt

Dystopia Series

Leashed

Caged

About the Author

Skye Warren is the New York Times and USA Today Bestselling author of dark romance. Her books are raw, sexual and perversely romantic.

Sign up for Skye's newsletter:
www.skyewarren.com/newsletter

Like Skye Warren on Facebook:
facebook.com/skyewarren

Follow Skye Warren on Twitter:
twitter.com/skye_warren

Visit Skye's website for her current booklist:
www.skyewarren.com

Copyright

Beauty Touched the Beast © 2011 by Skye Warren
Print Edition

Cover design by Book Beautiful
Formatting by BB eBooks

18202359R00023

Printed in Great Britain
by Amazon